Kittens! Kittens! Kittens!

Susan Meyers
illustrated by David Walker

Abrams Books for Young Readers, New York

ARTIST'S NOTE

My art is created entirely by hand using acrylic paint on paper. Each image begins with a pencil sketch, which is followed by the application of multiple layers of color to achieve depth and texture in the art.

Library of Congress Cataloging-in-Publication Data:
Meyers, Susan.
Kittens! Kittens! Kittens! / by Susan Meyers ;
illustrated by David Walker.
p. cm.
Summary: Illustrations and rhyming text portray kittens as
they go from nestling newborns to proud, independent,
and ready to have kittens of their own.
ISBN-13: 978-0-8109-1218-2
ISBN-10: 0-8109-1218-X
[1. Cats—Fiction. 2. Animals—Infancy—Fiction.
3. Stories in rhyme.] I. Walker, David, 1965– ill. II. Title.
PZ8.3.M5599Ki 2007
[E]—dc22
2006013575

Text copyright © 2007 Susan Meyers
Illustrations copyright © 2007 David Walker

Book design by Vivian Cheng
Production manager: Alexis Mentor

Printed and bound in China
10 9 8 7 6 5 4 3 2 1

HNA
harry n. abrams, inc.
a subsidiary of La Martinière Groupe

115 West 18th Street
New York, NY 10011
www.hnabooks.com

To Teri Sloat, who opened the door to rhyme
—S.M.

To Julie! You're wonderful!
—D.W.

Kittens black and kittens white,

Kittens spotted, kittens striped.

Fluffy, puffy, tiny kittens,
Slender, sleek, and shiny kittens.

Here and there and everywhere,
Kittens! Kittens! Kittens!

Newborn kittens, soft as silk,
Tummies filled with mother's milk.

Nestling, cozy, then at last—
Standing up and growing fast.

Finding tails to stalk and chase,
Washing whiskers, ears, and face.

Pouncing, bouncing, mewing kittens,
Busy, up-and-doing kittens.

Here and there and everywhere,

Kittens!

Kittens!

Kittens!

Kittens leaving all they've known,
Soon exploring brand-new homes.

Chasing toys that skip and skitter,

Trying out their kitty litter.

Hiding when they're feeling shy,
Glad to find a lap nearby.

Warm and snuggly,
cuddly kittens,
Pick-me-up-and-
hug-me kittens.

Here and there and everywhere,

Kittens! Kittens! Kittens!

Kittens growing brave and bold,

Hard to catch and hard to hold.

Climbing curtains, shredding chairs,
Ganging up on teddy bears.

Knocking knickknacks, crouched in sacks,
Leaping out in sneak attacks!

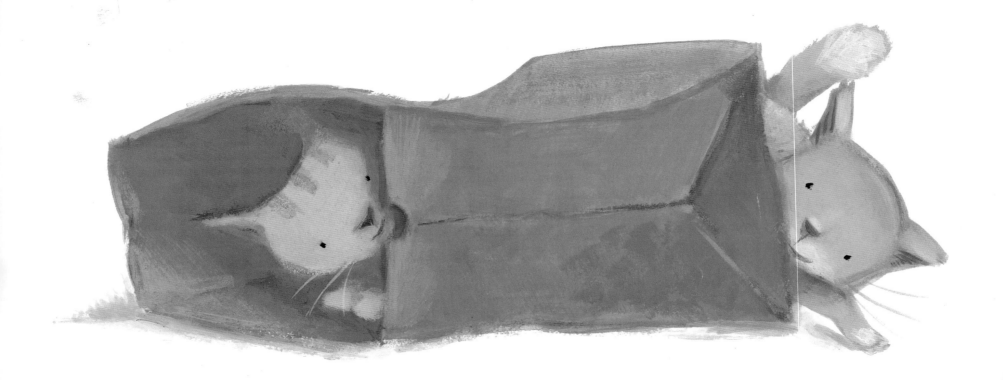

Reckless, wild, and crazy kittens,
Seldom ever lazy kittens.

Here and there and everywhere,
Kittens! Kittens!
Kittens!

Kittens getting bells to wear,

Scratching posts instead of chairs.

Learning where to climb and leap,
Choosing perfect spots to sleep.

Purring when they're stroked just so,
Free to come and free to go.

Smart and friendly,
    splendid kittens,
Proud and
    independent kittens.

Here and there and everywhere,

Kittens! Kittens! Kittens!

Kittens growing into cats,
Strong and nimble acrobats.

Chasing mice and rats away,

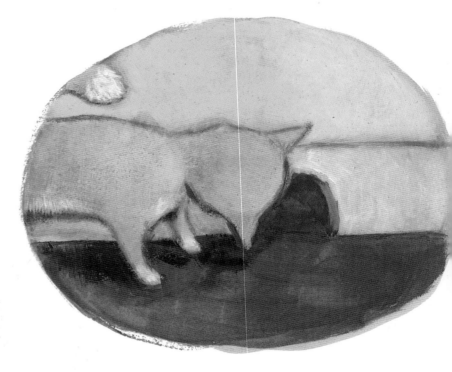

Taking catnaps through
the day.

Hiding, silent,
out of sight,
Keeping children
warm at night.

Watching, waiting,
making friends,
Perhaps becoming
parents, then . . .

Here and there and everywhere,
Kittens! Kittens! Kittens!